Christmas Tree

By *Thornton W. Burgess*

Pictures By *Mary and Carl Hauge*

WONDER BOOKS • NEW YORK
A Division of GROSSET & DUNLAP, Inc.

The Littlest Christmas Tree sighed. It was a soft, wistful sigh but, soft as it was, two pairs of long ears heard it. Peter Rabbit and his cousin, Jumper the Hare, were sitting under the green spreading branches of the Littlest Christmas Tree. They were so still the little tree had forgotten they were there.

The little tree began to whisper to itself.

"I wish . . ." whispered the Littlest Christmas Tree. Then it stopped to sigh, that same wistful little sigh.

"What do you wish?" asked Peter Rabbit, his long ears standing straight up.

"I wish I were tall," sighed the littlest tree. "I wish I were the tallest tree in all the Green Forest."

"Why?" asked Jumper the Hare. His long white ears with black tips also stood up. Curiosity often makes ears stand up—too often.

"So I could look down and see everything every-where," replied the Littlest Christmas Tree, and sighed again.

"Silly!" cried Peter Rabbit, laying his long ears back along his shoulders and settling himself comfortably. "Silly! What good would it do you to see everything everywhere?"

Just then Sammy Jay began to scream. "Thief! Thief! Thief!" screamed Sammy.

Peter's ears flew straight up again. "I wonder who Sammy is calling a thief this time," cried Peter. Away he went, lipperty, lipperty, lip, to see what was happening.

"And Peter thinks I'm curious because I want to see, too," sighed the littlest tree.

The little tree had time to sigh only twice be-
fore Peter Rabbit came running back faster than
ever. Behind him came Reddy Fox running just as
fast. His big tail was carried high and he was hand-
some indeed. In a moment, they had disappeared.

"I hope Peter will get away from Reddy Fox, but
how shall I ever know? Oh, how I wish I were the
tallest tree in the Green Forest! Then I could see
everywhere," sighed the little tree.

The next day a strange and dreadful thing happened. Men came and cut down all the young trees. Christmas was drawing near and these were Christmas trees. Sadly the tall trees nearby, safe because they were too big, watched the young trees fall in the soft snow. Then the trees were piled onto a great truck.

For a few minutes the littlest tree stood alone. Because it was not as tall as the others, it had not been cut. For the first time, the other trees were not in its way and the little tree could see all around. But there was nothing to see.

"This tree is small, but someone may want it," said a voice and an axe cut the little tree down.

"Caw, caw, caw! Too bad! Too bad!" called Blacky the Crow, flying high above the truck for a little way.

The trees were taken on a long journey to a great city by the sea. There, in the market place, the trees were sold one by one and carried away. They were all taken to lovely homes, and each tree brought into the home happiness and song and laughter and love. Only the littlest tree was left standing alone in the market place.

Then a man with a sun- and wind-browned face
came hurrying toward the market place. He saw the
little lone tree. The man bought it and carried it
aboard a great ship called a freighter. There the little tree was seemingly forgotten.

One day, a fussy little tugboat set its snub nose against the side of the great ship, and pushed it this way, and shoved it that way, and nudged it another way. At last the bow of the great ship was pointed straight for the open water of the sea. With a blast of her whistle, the great ship was on her way to distant lands.

Wound and bound with a cord, the little tree could not even sigh.

Then a wonderful thing happened. All in a day, the Littlest Christmas Tree became the tallest of all that had grown in the Green Forest. It was unbound and all its green branches were carefully spread out. It was hung with little bulbs of glittering colored glass. And then it was hoisted up and up—until it was at the very top of the tall foremast. "Now I can see everything everywhere," whispered the littlest tree to itself.

At first everything was strange. All the tree saw
was water everywhere—water as blue as the sky
itself. Then, looking down, the tree saw flying fish
rising out of the water around the ship's bow. They
glided low above the water, and then plunged back
into the blue depths.

After the flying fish disappeared, porpoises
rolled and tumbled around the bow of the ship.

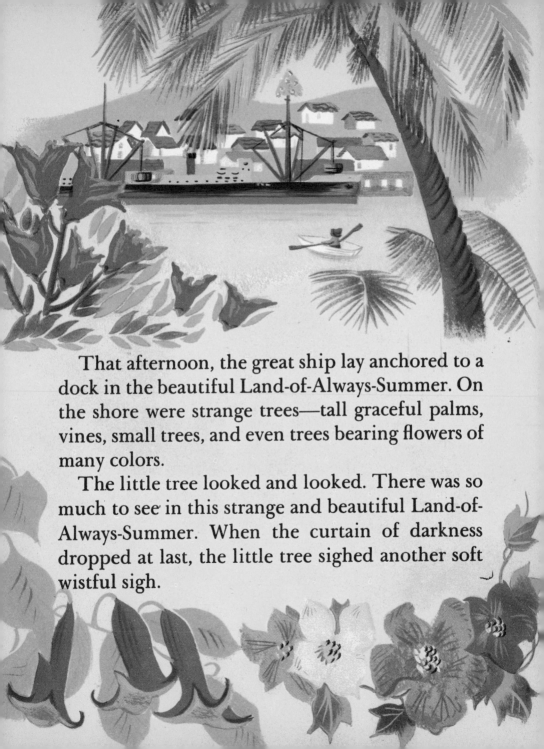

That afternoon, the great ship lay anchored to a dock in the beautiful Land-of-Always-Summer. On the shore were strange trees—tall graceful palms, vines, small trees, and even trees bearing flowers of many colors.

The little tree looked and looked. There was so much to see in this strange and beautiful Land-of-Always-Summer. When the curtain of darkness dropped at last, the little tree sighed another soft wistful sigh.

Then another wonderful thing happened. One
after another, lights sprang out here, there, and
everywhere—shining bright in the velvety black-
ness. Suddenly all the glass bulbs on the little tree

burst into colored lights. There were joyous shouts from the decks below and from the dock beyond. The happy voices of children mingled with the happy voices of men and women. There was music and dancing and song and laughter far into the night, for it was Christmas Eve.

When one by one the lights winked out, it seemed as if the lights on the Littlest Christmas Tree high on the foremast shone brighter than ever. Once more the little tree sighed ever so softly, but this time it was a sigh of joy.

For in the soft stillness of the tropic night, as among the snow-clad hills of its northern home, the spirit of peace and good will and love was settling over all the Great World.

Much later, a great light crept over the sky in the east. And the Littlest Christmas Tree watched the dawn of Christmas morning.